Sophie Washington
Mission Costa Rica

Written By
Tonya Duncan Ellis

Other Books by Tonya Duncan Ellis

Sophie Washington: Queen of the Bee

Sophie Washington: The Snitch

Sophie Washington:
Things You Didn't Know About Sophie

Sophie Washington: The Gamer

Sophie Washington: Hurricane

Table of Contents

Chapter 1

Welcome to the Jungle

The sky is sunglasses-required bright. It is hotter than a coal-fired pizza oven. Sweat drips into my eyebrows, and my t-shirt sticks to my back like gum to the underside of a desk. Ignoring the baking temperature, Carlos, our guide, is the one of the cheeriest people I've ever met. It's like a smile is tattooed on his mouth as we bump along the narrow, winding road at about ten miles per hour.

"Ev-er-y-body, stop!"

Carlos abruptly puts on the brakes and yells, still grinning, to get our attention. My dad jerks our golf cart to a halt right behind him.

It's Day One of our trip to Costa Rica, and Dad, Mom, my little brother Cole and my friends Chloe, Valentina, and I are taking a tour of the golf course near our hotel.

Ooo! Ooo! Ooo!

The exotic sounds of howler monkeys and sights of red, yellow and blue parrots, lime green iguanas, and tropical plants mingle with the common golfing fairways and tees.

"Whoa! Check that out over there!" Cole points out a thick, gray and forest green-colored hose sliding on the turf.

"What do we have here?" asks Carlos.

"Get back, kids!" Mom exclaims. "It's a snake!"

A five-foot-long serpent glides near Carlos' feet, and instead of moving away our crazy guide eases toward the creature.

I freeze. Everyone else steps back.

"Not to worry, the snake is not poisonous," Carlos reassures us. "It's a boa constrictor." Then he reaches down to pick it up and wraps the snake around his neck as we all stare with our mouths agape.

Smack!

Mosquitoes buzz toward my open lips and I whack at my mouth to stop them. I can't keep my eyes off the serpent. And it looks like he's checking me out too.

"Would you like to pet it, young lady?" Carlos inquires. "We see this snake on the path nearly every day; he won't hurt you."

"A boa constrictor's bite won't hurt you, but it can squeeze you to death," warns my father, holding his arms out to keep me from getting too close.

"I bet Sophie is part Slytherin, just like Harry Potter," says Cole, comparing me to the snake-loving members of the club from the Harry Potter book series while he observes the snake and me watch each other.

"Be quiet, Cole, and all you children stay back," scolds my mother.

I blink and the spell the snake cast on me is broken. I am able to move again.

"I can't believe we're this close to a boa constrictor," Valentina says as she snaps a picture of the snake-clad Carlos with her cell phone. "No one will believe this is real."

"Yeah, looking at that creepy thing makes my skin crawl." Chloe smooths a black curl off her forehead and peers to get a better look. "Take one of me standing with the snake in the background, Valentina," she asks, striking a pose.

I roll my eyes. Leave it to my two friends to be snapping selfies when we might be in danger. Though we are all on the cheerleading squad, Chloe Thompson and Valentina Martinez would probably be considered the most "high maintenance" in our group. Both love to shop and spend lots of time talking about hair and makeup. They are both very pretty too. Chloe is tall and thin with dark curls and caramel skin, and Valentina, who was born in Mexico, has long black hair and can do back flips across the school gym.

Chloe and I have been best friends since we were small. We've been in most classes together at Xavier Academy, the private school we attend, until last year when she was placed in some special classes

because she has dyslexia. The learning disorder makes her see letters backward so Chloe needs more time to do her reading assignments than other people. Some kids used to make fun of her about it until they found out that Chloe has a temper, and since she's one of the tallest girls in our grade you don't want to mess with her.

I used to think Valentina was just a bubblehead until she and her family had to leave their home during a hurricane earlier this year. They camped out with us in my father's dental office for a few days because parts of our neighborhood were flooding and we couldn't stay in our house either. During our time in the office, Valentina and I became friends and she convinced me to try out for the cheerleading team.

"Can I see the pictures?" Cole bumps me out of the way and shoves in closer. "I left my camera at the hotel."

"Ouch!" I stumble back off the path and into a huge pile of fire ants.

At least fifty angry bugs crawl up my leg and start biting.

"Aaaaah!" I shriek.

Mom rushes over and swats the ants off with her sun hat.

"Everybody back on the golf carts!" she commands.

"Is your daughter okay?" A lady from one of the two other carts touring with us walks over to offer help.

"Yes, thankfully, she's not allergic to fire ant venom," Mom answers. "It looks like she'll have to suffer through pain from a bite or two the next couple of days."

"A bite or two? There must be at least twenty bumps on my leg!" I exclaim. "And it's all your fault, Cole!"

Chapter 2

Trouble in Paradise

"Don't blame me," my brother retorts. "You should have been paying attention to where you were going instead of speaking the Harry Potter wizard language Parseltongue to that boa constrictor."

I hold back on shoving him because I know I'll end up in trouble here in paradise if I start fighting my little brother.

Some vacation. First, we find out that Costa Rica is just as hot, humid and buggy as our hometown in Houston, Texas, and now I get even more ugly bites on my leg than I'd get if I had stayed home. My Dad decided to bring us on this trip for spring break when a mission from our church asked him to come down for a week to give free dental service to the people who live here. Though it's a beautiful place, Costa Rica is a Third World country. Many of the people live in small huts and they don't get things that we take for granted like regular dental and doctor checkups.

My dad is a dentist, and my mother works with him in his office doing bookkeeping and helping make sure things run well. Dad thought coming on the mission trip would be a great way to help others and have a nice, cheap vacation for our family.

"Since we're saving money on plane and hotel costs, why don't you invite a couple of your friends?" he suggested.

"Can we bring Bertram?" my brother Cole asked about our pet Portuguese Water Dog.

"Mr. McEwan wants to keep him while we are gone," responded Mom. Bertram stayed with our elderly neighbor, Mr. McEwan, earlier in the year when we had to evacuate our home in Houston during a hurricane, and even though our dog chews up everyone's shoes, Mr. McEwan, fell in love with him. He lives alone, so I guess it's good Bertram can keep him company.

Chloe and Valentina jumped at the chance to join me on the trip. I wish our other good friend, Mariama, could have come too, but her parents are taking her to Disney World for spring break. I thought this trip to Guanacaste, Costa Rica was going to be more exciting than the vacation Mariama was taking, but right about now, I would kill for some mouse ears and a ride on those giant Disney teacups. Pictures I've seen on the Internet show palm tree-filled tropical beaches and hotels like mansions to stay in, but we are bunking in some smaller huts that the church mission provides near a beach that looks nothing like what they show online. The only tree I see looks as pitiful as the one from *A Charlie Brown Christmas*. And a huge iguana was scurrying near the front door of the hut I'm sharing with my friends when we arrived this morning. I'll bet he was running for his life from this place.

"It's only for a week, Sophie," said Mom when she saw me scrunching up my nose at the inside of the hut. "Think of it as being in summer camp."

The place seems clean enough, but the furniture looks like it was old when my grandmother Granny Washington was a kid. There are two bunkbeds, an old-fashioned television that has terrible reception and four rickety wicker chairs. The bathroom is tiny, with a toilet, no bathtub and a small vanity. An overweight person might get stuck in the shower. The air conditioner doesn't work great but at least there is a ceiling fan to get a breeze going.

I'm not a complete girly girl like Chloe, who brought a ginormous pink leather suitcase with at least 20 outfit changes for a one-week mission trip, but I like to be comfortable. In our house in Houston, I have my own room with my own big double bed, and I also have my own small bathroom. But I *am* excited about the chance to sleep in a bunk bed, and to spend extra time with my friends, so I'll stop complaining. Cole is sleeping in a rollout bed in the same room as our parents.

"It's not fair that Sophie gets to bring her friends with her while I have no one," he whined when my parents told him our bedding arrangements.

"She's in sixth grade and you're in second," answered Mom. "You can spend some special time with your friends when we get home, Cole. We're going to have a wonderful vacation helping others and enjoying Costa Rica."

After we settled into our rooms, we made our way to the hotel visitor's area, where they told us about the golf tour. The concierge said we might see monkeys and parrots, but she neglected to tell us about the snakes and fire breathing ants.

I rub on my hot and swollen leg to soothe the itching.

"Daaang, Sophie, your leg is muy malo!" says Valentina, looking down to get a better look. Though she was born in America, Valentina's family speaks Spanish at home and she adds in Spanish words to the conversation once in a while. This used to get on my nerves, but now I roll with it.

"Try rubbing this on your bites," suggests Carlos, holding out a thick green leaf.

"What's that?" I ask.

"Aloe," he replies. "It will help make your leg feel much better."

"Good idea, thanks, Carlos," my father says as he takes a piece of the broken leaf and rubs it on my calf. It does sting less and the small bumps don't feel as itchy as they did before.

We see more howler monkeys swinging from trees than I can count as we make our way back up the trail toward the hotel.

"Those howler monkeys are small, but that Ooo, Ooo, Ooo, noise they make sounds deep like gorillas," observes Chloe.

"It's spooky, isn't it?" I answer. "I'd hate to be in here after dark."

"Yeah," agrees Valentina. "You'd be in big trouble out in this jungle once the sun goes down."

Chapter 3

Night Owls

My parents let us play at the beach for a couple hours after the golf course tour is over. Chloe, Valentina, and I splash in the water and then make a huge sandcastle that we plan to last for our entire week here, until Cole tries to do a cartwheel and falls on it. We change clothes back at our huts, then have a great dinner of beans, fish, rice and fried plantains at a restaurant near our hotel.

"It was a simple meal but tasted as good as any fine restaurant in Houston," says Dad, patting his stomach happily. "Let's get back to our huts to turn in. In the morning, we'll join the rest of the team from our church at the clinic in Guaitil."

"GuaiWhat?" asks Cole.

"It's the village where the mission medical building is located," explains Dad. "That area known for making beautiful pottery, so I'm sure you'll see lots of souvenirs you might want to buy before we go home."

"I prefer shopping for clothes," says Chloe, twirling a charm bracelet on her wrist. "But maybe I'll find something my parents will like."

"Mi abuela didn't give me any extra money for souvenirs," says Valentina wistfully. Her family lost their home and all their belongings during the huge hurricane that came through our hometown a few months ago. She, her grandmother, or abuela, and her preschool brother, Hector, are staying with some friends from their church until they can save enough money to rent a new place.

"The first couple of days you young ladies will be too busy working to worry about shopping," says Mom, as we approach our huts, "and I brought a small allowance for all of you to take gifts back to your families." My mother helps us get out towels and soap for our showers and makes sure we are settled in while my father gets Cole cleaned up next door.

"Stay in the hut and lock the door," she warns as she steps out. "Don't open it for anyone. Dad and I have a key to get in. We're right next door, and you can use this room phone here on the nightstand to call if you need us for anything."

"Yes, ma'am" I give her a peck on the cheek and click the latch on the lock once she leaves.

"I wish we could have our cell phones," says Valentina, after the door shuts. My parents take my phone up every evening before bed and they told my friends' parents they had to abide by the same rule to come on the trip. Chloe doesn't use her phone that much, but Valentina loves to take pictures and post them on social media Internet sites.

Ooo, Ooo, Ooo! Howler monkey calls echo through the jungle as the darkness sets in outside.

"I'm glad I'm not out there," says Chloe peeking out the blinds. "Do you guys want to play a game?" she suggests.

"You aren't tired?" I ask yawning. We drove to the airport around 5:30 this morning and I am exhausted.

"I'm a night owl," Chloe answers. "Plus, I slept on the plane."

She pulls out a pack of Uno cards and we begin to play. After a couple of rounds, I bow out and lie down on the lower bunk. I try to follow the conversation as Chloe and Valentina talk about boys they like from our grade and Chloe's last trip to the mall, but I can barely keep my eyes open.

"I think Nathan Jones has a crush on you, Sophie," are the last words I hear one of them say as I drift off to a deep sleep.

Chapter 4

Monkey Business

Tap, tap, tap, tap.

A rapping sound, like fingers on a keyboard wakes me in the middle of the night.

What could it be?

I didn't think to ask Mom to pack my night-light, and the room is pitch-black.

Tap, tap, tap, tap.

There it goes again! I sit up in my bed.

Then the howler monkeys start outside.

Ooo! Ooo! Ooo!

Tap, tap, tap, tap, sounds louder inside our hut.

"Valentina! Chloe!" I call out to my friends. My heart feels like it's ready to burst out of my chest. What could that noise be? There's something on the ground, near my bed. I don't want to step on the floor because I'm scared it might get me.

"Chloe! Valentina! Wake up!" I try again.

There's a rustle, then movement.

Eww! Eww! Eww! comes a sound near the ceiling.

What is going on?!!

My friends are still out like lights, so I reach for the cordless phone that is on the nightstand and hurl the receiver across the room to Chloe's bunk.

"Ouch!" she sits up. "Why'd you do that?"

"I hear a noise in here!!" I hiss. "Listen…"

Eww! Eww! starts the strange creature's cry.

Chloe, always the brave one, hops out of her twin bed and rushes to the light switch.

"Be careful, Chlo!"

I huddle on the bed with my arms wrapped around my legs, then squint at the blinding light.

Swinging from the ceiling fixture is a white-faced monkey.

"Ahhhhhh!" my friend and I screech.

Valentina rouses and starts to scream with us.

"Help! A monkey is trying to get us!!!"

I pound on the wall, hoping that my parents will hear us in their hut next door. The monkey swoops down from the ceiling fan and grabs the phone I threw on Chloe's bed.

"How did that thing get in here?" Valentina asks, jumping from her top bunk to join me and Chloe in my bed.

Ooo! Ooo! Ooo!

The howler monkeys outside shriek louder than ever. The monkey inside our hut beats the phone on his chest in answer to their calls.

"Mommy! Daddy!" I cry. I'm terrified to go out in the jungle after dark to find my parents. But I'm also scared stiff to stay in this room with Curious George.

"We've got to get him out of here," says Chloe.

The monkey holds the phone to his ear and starts jabbering like he's having a conversation.

"If we could get the phone from him, we could call your parents to let them know what's going on," says Valentina.

The clock on the wall says it's two a.m., so I know they probably won't hear us yelling. When Cole is in their room, my mother puts earplugs in because he sucks his thumb at night and she doesn't like to hear the slobbering noise. Dad sleeps so soundly that a freight train could run through the house without him waking up. We've got to get the phone!

"Hey that's mine!" Chloe calls out as our primate guest snaps one of her red hair barrettes in the tuft of fur on its head.

"I guess it's a girl!" giggles Valentina.

"Ooo. Ooo. Ooo," the monkey continues its phone conversation while we look on.

"Wonder who she's talking to? King Kong?" laughs Valentina.

"This is not funny, Valentina," I cry. "That thing could hurt us."

"It's too bad your parents took our cell phones from us," Chloe laments. "Then we could just call them over here."

"I know, right," I sigh.

Three minutes go by, and it seems like forever. Then Valentina gets an idea.

"Grab my backpack by the end of the bed, Chloe," she calls.

Chloe follows her orders and slides the forest green bag over to the edge of the bed.

"I have something in here our friend might like." Valentina pulls out a small banana.

"Mi abuela tells me to always keep a snack in case of emergencies," she says. "I guess having a monkey in our room counts."

"Be careful," I caution. "What if it attacks you?"

"She doesn't look too mean," Valentina says, assuming it's a girl because the monkey is still wearing Chloe's barrette. She waves the piece of fruit. "Over here, little monkey," she coos.

The monkey stops chattering on the phone and watches Valentina's banana, fascinated.

"Lead it out of here, Valentina," I call anxiously.

Chloe and I scoot closer together as Valentina eases off the bed and starts walking backward towards the hut's door.

Ooo! Ooo! Ooo!

Transfixed, the monkey follows her new leader and begs for the banana.

Suddenly, the hut door swings open.

"Ahhhhhh!" the three of us scream again in shock.

The monkey leaps out the doorway into the night.

Chapter 5

Guaitil

"What is going on in here!" my father demands shining a flashlight. "Are you girls alright?"

"There was a monkey in our hut, Dad." I rush off the bed to hug him. "It just ran out of here when you opened the door."

"A monkey!" my father exclaims. "How could it have gotten in here?"

He examines our living quarters as we huddle on my bed in relief that the intruder is gone.

"I don't see any entry points," says my father after a few minutes. "He must have been in the room all along or sneaked in with you after dinner."

"We think it's a girl," says Chloe, "because it put my red barrette in its fur."

"I'm guessing she was living here before we came," I add. "We didn't leave the door open or anything when we came in."

"Well, things seem secure now," says Dad. "Why don't you ladies get back to sleep?"

Ooo! Ooo! Ooo! scream howler monkeys outside in the jungle. My friends and I look at each other, wide eyed.

"We're scared to sleep here alone, Dad," I say. "Can we go in your hut?"

"I can understand why you'd be uneasy, Sophie," Dad comes to the bed and cuddles me close.

"Is everything okay?" Mom rushes to the doorway. "It was taking you so long to come back that I was getting worried."

"A monkey was in here," Dad explains. "It looked like those capuchin monkeys you see with street vendors or in the circus. He got active once the lights were out and scared the girls. When I opened the door to check on them, he ran away."

"Thanks goodness you weren't hurt!" my mother exclaims. "Why don't I stay in here with the girls, honey, and you go back with Cole?"

"Sounds like a plan," my father agrees. "See you bright and early in the morning. We've got plenty of work to do in the village."

"I don't know if I can go back to sleep after all this excitement," I say after my father closes the door.

"I'd better make sure I put my favorite head-bands up before he comes back and snags one of them too," jokes Chloe.

My friends get back in their beds, and Mom tucks them in.

"I know that must have been frightening," my mother soothes. "But capuchin monkeys generally aren't considered dangerous. In fact, I read that some are trained to help disabled people."

"Well if he got in here, other creatures could too," I fret. "What if that snake we saw on the golf course comes back?"

"I wish I could have taken a picture of it with my phone to post on Instapic," says Valentina. "That was cool watching the monkey hold the phone like she was making a call."

Mom squeezes in the twin bed with me and holds me close until I drift off again.

When I wake up, it's morning. Mom's gone, and Valentina and Chloe are still asleep.

"Come on guys, wake up," I shake them. "We've got to get ready for breakfast."

"Aie, aie aie, Sophie, give us a break." whines Valentina, pulling the blanket back over her head.

"Part of our vacation is helping the people in the village, remember?" I continue jostling my friend.

"All right, already," grumbles Chloe, rolling off her bunk bed and stumbling to the bathroom.

I can understand why my friends are cranky. I feel like I've been through a hurricane after all the drama we had last night with our new monkey friend. I rummage through my suitcase for my shorts and favorite blue t-shirt, and then grab my comb and brush to braid my hair.

Ten minutes after I wake the other girls up, Mom opens the door.

"Rise and shine, ladies! It's time to get a quick breakfast and head to the village to work! Are you feeling okay? That was quite the adventure you had last night."

"Yes, Ma'am," answer my friends.

"Does that mean you are okay, or that you had an adventure?" she chuckles.

"Both," says Valentina, lacing her sneakers. "Can we have our cell phones back?"

"Sure," says my mother, reaching to get them from her bag. "In light of what happened last night, I guess we should make sure you girls have your phones when your father and I aren't around. Of course, the cell phone service isn't great back here in the jungle. Regardless, I'll be staying with you in the night from now on, so you'll always have an adult around."

Great. My plan to have a giant parent-free sleepover for a week is ruined. But I guess it's a good price to pay to feel safe.

"I wish I could have seen the monkey!" Cole exclaims when we meet up with him and my father at their hut. "Sophie has all the fun."

"I wouldn't exactly call being awakened in the middle of the night by a wild monkey, fun," I answer. We head to the main area of the hotel to get something to eat before we go to work in the Guaitil medical center.

"What do they have for breakfast?" asks Cole. "Can we get the bacon and omelet buffet?"

"We got a late start this morning," says Dad. "We'll probably just get some cereal or something quick, so we're not late to help out. The people from the mission told me they'll have lunch for us at the site each day, which will be nice."

We fill bowls with cereal to take to our table and I also grab some yogurt and a piece of toast.

Valentina and Chloe perk up during breakfast and start taking selfies.

"The Wi-Fi here works great," Valentina says.

Now that they are awake, my friends start talking about what they love best, clothes and boys.

I blush when they mention Nathan Jones again. He's a boy in our class who I once nicknamed "Mr. Know-It-All." We used to hate each other when we competed in the school spelling bee in fifth grade last year. But things changed when Nathan helped me stand up to a bully later in the school year and we've been friends since, with the key word being "friends." The thought of him liking me is just icky. It's not that he's so horrible looking, though he wears glasses and is one of the shortest boys in our grade. I wear glasses too, but just to see the board in class. I just don't think of Nathan that way. The only boy I ever had a crush on was Toby Johnson, who plays on the basketball team, and he likes Chloe. I thought that being away for a week with my friends would give me a break from all the boy crazy nonsense but no such luck, I guess.

"Let's get a move on kids," says Dad tossing his juice carton in the trash and moving toward the eating area exit. Valentina and Chloe clear up their places at the table. Thankfully, the talk about Nathan Jones stops. I'd be mortified if my parents, or worse, Cole, hear what my friends were saying. I'd never hear the end of it.

Cole tells a joke as we make our way to the shuttle bus.

"Why is it hard to play cards in the jungle? There are too many cheetahs!"

"That's a good one, Cole," says Chloe, laughing.

"Please, don't encourage him," I warn.

The 20-minute drive to Guaitil is so bumpy it makes our ride on the golf carts yesterday seem like we were gliding on smooth ice.

Once we arrive at the village, my mother stands and rubs her bottom. "I will need to bring a pillow to sit on for our ride tomorrow."

"Mooom!" I blush in embarrassment.

My friends giggle.

Guaitil is a cute little village surrounded by lush tropical trees in the distance. There are several houses in the town square with open air areas filled with beautiful rust colored pottery. The pottery bowls and vases have black designs with pretty carvings of monkeys, turtles, parrots and other Costa Rican creatures and scenes.

"Wow, look at that!" Cole exclaims, pointing at an artisan sitting behind a pottery wheel at a table full of large bowls.

"Did you make all those?" he asks the man.

The artist looks at us and smiles.

"I'm not sure if he speaks English," says my father.

"Cuánto por los cuencos?"

Valentina asks how much the bowls cost in Spanish.

"Treinta dólares," the man answers.

"That's thirty dollars!" says Cole. "We learn our Spanish numbers in school."

"That's great, sweetie!" praises Mom.

The man begins to create a new bowl by spinning clay around on the pottery wheel.

"This is so cool!" exclaims Valentina, pulling out her phone and snapping a picture.

Cole spies a handmade whistle shaped like a parrot near some of the bowls and starts to blow on it.

"Put that down, son!" my father chastises him. He asks the man the price and hands him a $10 bill.

"Señor Washington! I am happy to see you and your family have arrived safely!" a short, pudgy man with a friendly face and a white beard and mustache rushes down the street to greet us. "The villagers are excited to have someone here to offer dental treatment. Let me show you to the clinic."

My father introduces the man as Father Ricardo Lopez. He is a priest who invited members of our church to volunteer at the mission. Father Lopez shows us a hut where some nice looking ladies are preparing what looks like a feast for us for lunch. I see large platters of beans, rice, chicken, plantains and vegetables, and some other things that may be desserts.

"Hola!" Valentina and Chloe wave and smile, and the women look up from their cooking to wave back. My stomach is grumbling already, and I can't wait to sample all the goodies at lunchtime.

Cole blows a tune on his whistle as we walk to the clinic. *This vacation is turning out better than I thought.*

Chapter 6

Hard Knock Life

I snap out of my happy feeling quicker than Cole takes a shower when Mom and Dad aren't looking, once we turn the corner.

A mile-long line of men, women and children snakes around the mission medical building. Many of them have rags wrapped around their heads, and some are moaning in pain.

This may be a long day.

"Do you have to take care of all those people, Daddy?" I ask.

"Dr. Washington! Boy, are we glad to see you!!" a young red-haired lady in scrubs with an English accent and a name tag that says "Greta" rushes across the courtyard to greet us. "These people have been lined up since sunrise to get treated by a trained dentist. Many of them have been suffering with toothaches and dental problems for months."

"We're glad to be here and are ready to work hard," says Mom after shaking Greta's hand and telling her all our names.

Dad goes into the medical facility to get started and Greta instructs us on our duties.

"We've been having some trouble with the water system, which should be repaired tomorrow. This morning, we need you kids to bring in as many buckets of fresh water as you can from the well back behind the building."

"What's a well?" asks Cole.

"It's a deep hole in the ground where they used to get all their water from in olden times," I answer.

"Some people still use them for water in modern times, as well," chuckles Greta. "Many of the people here in the village don't have running water."

"They're really in the dark ages around here, aren't they?" whispers Chloe.

"All right, let's get to it!" my mother says in a chipper voice. Greta brings out five metal buckets.

"Fill these up to the brim with water and pour it in the trough by the back door of the building," she instructs.

We immediately start working.

The first four trips to the well aren't so bad, but by the fifth, I'm ready to call it quits. The sun is scorching, the water-filled buckets are way heavier than they look, and the bug bites on my leg are starting to itch.

"When can we take a break, Mom?" Cole whines, and for once, I'm with him.

Both Chloe and Valentina's faces are red, and they look to my mother expectantly.

"How about you kids take a ten-minute breather, while I go get some more sunscreen and water bottles for you to drink?" she suggests. "Don't drink the well water."

Before coming to Costa Rica my parents warned us about getting sick to our stomachs from drinking Costa Rican water. It's not purified in the same way water is at home and since our bodies aren't used to it, it might make us sick.

"Thank you, Mrs. Washington!" Chloe readjusts her thick curls in her hair tie to get some relief from the heat. We sit on a stoop to rest while my mother gets our drinks.

"This work is really tough," says Valentina.

"Yeah, it's like we're doing hard labor like those kids in that *Annie* play we saw in our school musical last year," Chloe adds.

My brother, who seems to know every scene in every kid movie or song ever invented, starts to sing:

It's a hard knock life for us.
It's a hard knock life for us.
Steada treated we get tricked!
Steada kisses we get kicked!
It's a hard knock life!

My friends and I almost fall off the stoop from laughing.

"Children! Stop that nonsense!'" Mom scolds, striding up with four icy bottles of water. "It's a good thing most of these people don't speak English. They are grateful we are here to help them. We have things so good back home. Let's not complain about serving others."

"Yes, ma'am." We settle down, slather up with sunscreen and bug repellent, drink our water, and get back to hauling buckets.

Thankfully, the lunch the women from the village make us is even better than it looks because I don't know if I would be able to make it to the four o'clock quitting time without passing out if I didn't have something filling in my stomach.

"You children are doing a wonderful job and should be proud of yourselves," says my mother as we shove tasty empanada pastries filled with meat and cheese, rice and beans in our mouths.

My father doesn't eat lunch with us because he's so busy, but he does stop by our table to thank us for all we are doing to help.

"I've seen patients this morning and pulled out a tooth from one lady who had been in pain for six months," he said. "I hope I can get to all the people who need dental care before we leave at the end of the week. They have come from miles around to see us."

"It feels wonderful to be able to bless other people like this," Mom exclaims.

Our hearty lunch gives us a burst of energy. We move almost twice as many buckets of water before our 4 p.m. quitting time.

"Thanks again for all the help," Greta tells us as we are gathering our things to leave. "You children did a marvelous job. We would have had to send all these people home today if you hadn't been here to haul the water. The workers are almost complete with the plumbing, so we will have another job for you tomorrow."

"I feel grateful to be able to help," answers Mom.

"We do too," chime in my friends.

"And me four," pipes up Cole.

Chapter 7

House Guest

The van ride back to our hotel is relatively quiet, since all four of us kids doze off from exhaustion after doing such hard work in the hot sun.

I'm so tired I barely notice the many jolts and bumps we experience on the unpaved road.

"Look, everybody!" Cole's loud voice wakes me from my nap as we approach our hut.

An animal with a small flash of red on its head is swinging through the trees.

"It's the monkey from our room!" exclaims Chloe "and she's still wearing my barrette!"

Ewww, ewww, ewww! cries the primate.

"I hope it doesn't try to get back in our hut tonight," I shiver.

"There's no chimney for it to climb down, but I'll check all the areas near the roof again to be sure," my father reassures. "I let the hotel staff know what was going on before we had breakfast so

I'm sure they inspected as well. I suspect the monkey must have gotten in your hut when they cleaned from the last guests and stayed until we got here."

The monkey disappears into the jungle, and we go in our hut to clean up and change into our bathing suits for a swim.

"Wait for me, Sophie!" calls Cole as Valentina, Chloe and I scurry down the paved path to the pool.

We splash and float for about an hour before meeting my parents at the hotel's casual outdoor restaurant for dinner. It's a festive place with bright, orange, yellow and hot pink table cloths. My stomach rumbles as I smell the delicious scents of hot and spicy dishes. Once we are seated at a table overlooking the water my father praises us again.

"You kids did a phenomenal job at the mission today and many of the people from the group remarked at how well behaved you were. I sure am proud of your good attitudes and how you are really making a difference."

"Thanks, Dad," I answer. "It is fun to help other people."

"Yeah, and I can feel my muscles getting stronger and stronger from lifting those heavy buckets," boasts Cole.

We eat fried Mahi Mahi fish, rice and green salad until we are stuffed. We were all so hungry that Cole and I don't complain about having vegetables like we do at home. The sun starts to set around 5:30 p.m. and we watch in awe when the sky turns pink, then orange, with flashes of fiery red, and even purple, as the sun sinks beneath the ocean waves.

"Everything is so pretty here," says Valentina with appreciation.

"Why does it get dark so soon in Costa Rica, Dad?" asks Cole. At home, we're still able to ride our scooters outside in bright light in the springtime until well past 7 p.m.

"The seasons in Costa Rica are opposite ours in Houston," my father explains. "It's fall here while it's spring at home. And their summer is our winter."

"No fair! That means they have summer vacation while we are still in class." Cole frowns.

"But the children here are taking classes now, while you are on break," says my mother "Remember those school kids we saw holding books when we were in the van this morning?"

Ooo, ooo, ooo!

When nightfall comes, the howler monkeys start up their racket again, but I'm too tired to worry about last night's visitor returning. My friends must be worn out as well because they don't play with their cell phones much and start snoring shortly after my mother turns out the lights.

Tap, tap, tap.

I wake up again around 11 p.m. to the familiar tapping sound. *Not again!*

"Mom!" I whisper loudly. "Mom! Can you hear me?"

"What is it, dear?" my mother asks from the bunk above me.

"I think the monkey is back."

Chloe and Valentina are still snoring in the bunkbeds beside ours.

We listen for about five minutes. The room remains silent.

"I don't hear anything, Sophie," says my mother. "Maybe you were having a nightmare."

"I know I heard it, Mom!" I protest.

"Let's wait and see, honey," my mother answers. "I don't want to turn the lights on and wake the other girls. We have another busy day tomorrow, and none of us got a full night's sleep last night."

I stay alert for the next ten minutes. There is no other noise besides the howler monkeys outside, my friends' snores and my mother's soft breathing. I start to drift off again.

A half hour goes by, and I open my eyes to see light shining through the window blinds. A sinewy shape is moving in the air beside my bed. It's the boa constrictor from the golf course!

I gasp, too spellbound to make a sound. Once again, the snake's yellow eyes bore into mine. I feel like I am frozen in time and can't move. I open my mouth to scream, but no sound comes out. It's like I'm muffled, drowning in water or about to suffocate. The snake slithers closer to me, coiling near my body, ready to grip my neck and tighten. I flinch as I anticipate the feel of its cold scaly body on my skin.

"Nooooo! Help somebody! Heeelp!!"

I yell loudly as the sound I struggled to release comes out. Then I sneeze.

"Sophie, what's going on?" Chloe rubs her eyes in the twin bed beside mine.

I sit up, realizing it was all a dream.

"I thought that boa constrictor we saw the other day was in here and was trying to choke me," I shiver.

"Girls, you need to go back to sleep," mumbles my mother. "We are going to be exhausted in the morning."

Tap, tap, tap.

I hear the sound again!

"Did you hear it this time?" I hiss.

Tap, tap, tap. Tap!

"Yes, the monkey's back!" exclaims Chloe. She bravely gets up and flicks on the light switch again.

Ewww! Ewww! Ewww! the monkey cries.

"Not again!" Valentina pulls her pillow over her head.

"How does that thing keep getting in here?" wonders Chloe.

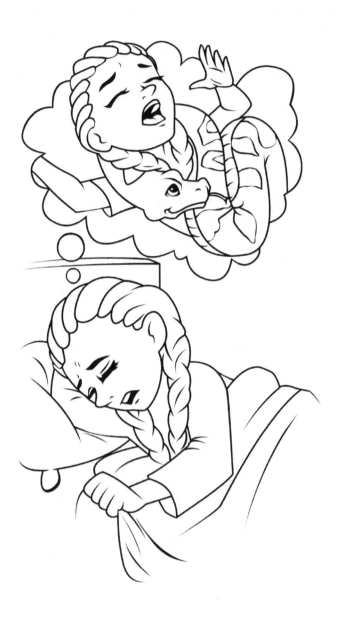

"It must have been in my bed!" I exclaim, seeing a fluff of fur on my covers. "That's what made me sneeze. I thought it was the boa constrictor, but it was the monkey!"

The creature swings to the nightstand, but Chloe grabs up the telephone receiver before it can swipe it again.

"You need to find a pay phone to make your calls on, Ms. Monkey," Chloe scolds.

Aggravated, the primate snatches a glittery headband that Chloe left on the table.

"He's taking more of my stuff!" she cries.

"That monkey is unwelcome company at this time of night," my mother complains. "Come on let's find something to lure it out of the hut. Anyone have any snacks?"

Valentina pulls out some crackers she'd stashed in her bag at the restaurant and my mother scatters a trail of them, Hansel and Gretel-style, leading to the door of our hut.

"Here, girl," she calls in a sing-song voice, like she uses to talk to our dog Bertram.

As the primate hesitantly gathers the midnight snack, Valentina takes a photo with her cell phone.

The monkey follows the food outside the doorway and mom slams the door shut.

"Bye, bye!" laughs Chloe.

Eww! Eww! Eww! our expelled guest cries angrily.

"How did it get back in here?" I ask. "And what if it comes back?"

"Those are good questions, Sophie," my mother answers. "There must be some opening on the roof that the monkey is using to get in. We may have to change our living quarters tomorrow. I doubt it will come back in the room tonight. Let's try to get some rest."

"Can I sleep with you, Mom?" I ask. My mother sighs and lets me lie at her feet while she sleeps on the other end of my twin bed. My friends don't seem scared and are back to snoring within a few minutes.

At first light, Mom calls the hotel maintenance crew to come out and inspect our room again.

"A hinge on the rooftop is loose, señora," says the repairman. "That is probably how el mono got in your hut. We will make the repairs this afternoon to solve the problem. I'm so sorry for your discomfort."

Chapter 8

Agnese

"This trip is certainly turning out to be full of adventure, isn't it?" asks my father when we meet him and Cole outside our huts after dressing and describe our second visit from our houseguest.

Cole grumbles again about missing out. "I wish I could switch rooms!"

I yawn.

Two days of excitement and activity combined with two nights of little sleep are starting to take their toll. I see mom drinking coffee during breakfast and wish I could have a cup.

"What's on our agenda today, Mr. W?" asks Chloe. She is wearing a bright, orange-colored t-shirt, jean shorts and a Houston Astros baseball cap this morning to shade her head from the broiling sun.

"I'll be back in the clinic, and I think they want you kids to help out with food prep."

"Yay!" I pump my fist in the air. I'm happy that we won't have to be outside or do any heavy lifting today.

"That's the first time I've seen you this excited about doing work," chuckles my mother.

"What I'm happy about is being in AC," I reply.

My cool air dreams are dashed once we arrive at the campsite. The kitchen is even hotter than it is outside because the ovens are going. And there is neither air conditioning, nor a fan.

"We need you children to assist with cleaning dishes and chopping onions and peppers for the evening meal," says Greta. She leads us to the food prep area where we saw the ladies making our lunches yesterday.

The sweet ladies who waved at us are gone. In their place is a younger, thinner woman around my mother's age, who is scowling.

"Good morning, Señora Alvarez," says Greta. "These children and their mother are here to help you in the kitchen."

"Buenos dias," says Valentina politely.

I know that means "Good Day" in Spanish, but it seems like Señora Alvarez got up on the wrong side of the tamale truck this morning. She is *not* happy that we are in the kitchen with her and has no problem showing it, slamming pots around the kitchen and scowling.

"Where are all the people we saw cooking yesterday?" I ask.

"Serving meals at another worksite," says Greta. "Some of the food they prepped can be heated and eaten today. But we need you to clean up the kitchen from this morning's dishes and help get things ready for the evening meal."

"No, no, no!" Señora Alvarez frowns, shaking her head as I attempt to cut up onions with a dull knife. "Make the pesos smaller."

"I think she means 'pieces,'" whispers Chloe as I look around in confusion.

I realize that Mrs. Alvarez is not talking too much to us because her English isn't great.

This kitchen feels warmer now than it did when we came in. Chloe takes her orange baseball cap off and Valentina chugs more from her water bottle. I don't know how the cooks who work here every day can stand it.

I see my mother giggling as my friends and I start tearing up from the onion fumes.

"I'll never get this smell off my hands," Chloe complains.

Cole is having fun playing in the water as he attempts to scrub pans until Señora Alvarez comes around fussing at him in Spanish.

"I wish I had my cell to take a photo of this," laughs Valentina, watching Cole cower. "Mrs. Alvarez doesn't play."

Once we finish cutting up a huge vat of onions, we help make empanadas. Though it's roasting in the hot kitchen, it's fun learning to roll the dough and shape the small pastries that will be filled with meat, cheese, corn and other savory goodies.

"Mamá, can I help?" a girl who looks not much older than Cole comes into the kitchen.

"Why are you not in school, child?" Mrs. Alvarez frowns.

"We have a half day today, remember? Since the tooth doctor is here. Our teacher is letting the kids out early this week in case they need to get their teeth checked."

"That's just for the children who need to go," Mrs. Alvarez answers. "Your teeth are fine."

Mrs. Alvarez starts speaking quickly in Spanish, and I can't understand what she is saying. I look to Valentina to translate.

"The girl is asking if we are American and if she can help us in the kitchen," she whispers.

"We would love for you to help us if your mother says it's okay," pipes up Chloe, rubbing her onion-stained hands on a dish towel.

"Can I stay, mama?" the little girl begs. "Practicing my English with real Americans is better than learning in school."

Mrs. Alvarez grudgingly nods her approval and her daughter hugs her.

"Muy bien!" she exclaims smiling and looks over at our work. "I don't know how to make many things, but my empanadas are pretty good. My name is Agnese. What are yours?"

We introduce ourselves and Agnese tells us about her school life in Guaitil. She is ten years old and plays on the soccer team. Agnese has five brothers and three sisters, but they are all older than her and have their own children.

"When I grow up I want to visit America and maybe go to college there," she says.

"If you want to go to college than you need to stay in school the whole day and not sneak out to spy on Americans," scolds Mrs. Alvarez.

"My family is originally from Mexico," shares Valentina. "My grandmother and parents moved to America a few years ago, but my parents had to go back to Mexico because they didn't have approval from the government to stay."

I feel bad for Valentina because it's been over two years since she's seen her mom and dad. Her grandmother is saving money so they can take a trip to Mexico in the summer.

The cooking goes much faster with Agnese chattering about her school and asking us questions about life in America.

"Do you go to New York City a lot?" she asks us. "I want to visit the Empire State Building and Times Square."

"New York is far away from where we live," answers Cole. "We're from Houston, Texas."

Cole describes Xavier Academy, the private school we attend, and tells Agnese how he rode a sheep in a muttin' bustin' contest at the Houston Livestock and Rodeo show last year.

"Wow, you are like a Western cowboy!" she exclaims.

Soon it is time for us to head back to our hotel.

"Do you have a computer?" I ask Agnese. "Maybe we can email you when we get home."

"Or you could exchange addresses and write each other letters," interrupts my mom.

"We do have a computer class at school," Agnese replies. "I will ask my teacher if I can use it to send you messages."

I give her my email, and my home address, just in case.

"Hasta luego, Agnese," says Valentina. "I hope we'll see you before we leave Costa Rica."

"See you later," she replies.

Chapter 9

Zip Line

We take the next day off from work.

"Doctors are doing physicals in the clinic today so the dental group doesn't need to go in," my father explains.

Our friend the monkey did not return to our hut in the evening and we were able to get a good night's sleep.

"The hotel staff sealed up the hole in the hut roof while we were gone yesterday, which must have done the trick," guesses my mother.

"I'm grateful for that," says Chloe, heading to the bathroom to wash up. "If that monkey comes back too many more times I won't have anything to fix my hair with. He got away with my favorite headband the other night."

"I'm glad I got some good pictures of it," says Valentina. "I think your barrette shows in one of them, Chloe."

At breakfast, our father tells us about our plans for the day.

"I signed us up for a zip lining excursion."

"What's that?" asks Cole.

"It's a ride where they strap you up to a cable, hundreds of feet up in the air, and you swing over the trees," explains Valentina. "I did it with my mother and father one time in Mexico."

My father pulls out the brochure and shows it to us.

"We'll do 10 total zip lines and one will go over a river," he reads.

Are they serious? I threw up earlier this year on a giant slide at the Spring Spectacular festival at school because I was afraid of being up so high. There's no way I'm swinging through the trees like Tarzan.

The ever-brave Chloe also looks nervous.

"Is this safe?" she asks.

"It's one of the most popular tourist activities here in Costa Rica," says my father. "They strap you securely onto the cable so there is no way for you to fall off. It's a great way to get a spectacular view of the jungle and maybe even the ocean."

"Yay! We'll be swinging through the trees like monkeys!" cheers Cole.

"You'll love it, Chlo," agrees Valentina.

Like me, Chloe doesn't look convinced.

"Let's see what it's like when we get there, and if you children don't feel comfortable you won't have to participate," assures Mom.

It takes us about twenty minutes to get to the zip line place from our hotel, but it feels like a million years to me because I'm so nervous. The zip line center is located on a farm that also has horse riding jungle tours.

"Cool! I've always wanted to ride a horse," says Chloe watching some riders trot in.

"What street do horses live on?" jokes Cole. "Mane Street."

I groan feeling more agitated as we walk closer to the zip line area. "Cole, you are not even funny!"

Before we can zip line, we have to go through safety training and watch a video on what not to do. My folks sign waiver forms saying the zip line place is not responsible if anything happens to us. You'd think this would make them aware that this is not a great idea, but no such luck.

"Do not put your hands on the zip line cable to stop yourself," warns the video announcer.

"That's the surest way to get injured," adds Diego, one of our guides. "Your finger could get cut off. Pull on the brake on the cable to stop yourself, and we can help stop you as well if you are having any trouble."

"You're going to love this, kids!" enthuses Dad after Diego hands out special belts, gloves and helmets for us to put on. "Zip lining is something that's always been on my bucket list."

"Bucket list?" I ask.

"Things I want to do before I pass away," my father responds.

Pass away?!! He is not making this anymore appealing to me.

Mom double checks us kids to make sure we have our gear on securely. The belts are made of a thick material like you see on car seatbelts and they wrap around our waists and legs. We have metal clamps on our belts that will hook us onto the zip lines and we're wearing bandana scarves on our heads under our helmets.

I pull at the flimsy straps. This definitely doesn't feel as safe as riding a ride at an amusement park. Once again, I wish I could trade places with our friend Mariama, who is spending spring break in Disney World.

"Cole, come and take our picture!" asks Valentina, grabbing Chloe and me in for a hug.

I plaster on a smile, though my heart still isn't in this. I don't want to spoil the fun for everyone, but I just don't want to go.

"You all right, honey?" My father grabs my hand as we drive up a steep hill in a mini bus to make our way to the zip line platforms.

I lie and nod my head. The knot in my stomach gets tighter and tighter each mile higher we climb. The mini bus drops us off at the bottom of a platform and we start making the steep hike up the mountain. Though it's high up to the top, the hike isn't as hard as I thought. The thick vegetation makes it feel like its air conditioned so we're not as hot as we've been on other days of our trip. Valentina, Chloe, and Cole point out a family of iguanas on the side of the path.

"That one's moving near a banana tree!" Cole calls excitedly, pointing at the small fragrant tree loaded with yellow and light green fruit.

As we make our ascent, our guides Jose and Diego chatter away in Spanish. If I didn't think they'd hear me, I'd ask Valentina what they are saying. Once we stop, Jose turns to talk to us. "All right fam-i-lee! Since we're near the platforms, the only way down is through the zip lines. The buses cannot reach us, so get ready to swing!"

Now they tell me! There's no way to get out of doing this!!

My heart flutters faster when we arrive at the first zip line area and I look down at the green rainforest below.

"Whoa! That's a looooong way down!!" Cole exclaims.

"Almost four hundred feet," clarifies Diego.

"It's just beautiful, isn't it?" my mother beams and squeezes my hand.

I hear birds and other animals calling in the breeze. My heart feels like its beating louder than the jungle cries.

Diego clamps himself onto the zip line cable to give a live demonstration. In less than two minutes, he speeds to the other side of the platform, holding his arms out and flipping upside-down midway through the ride.

"Up, up and away!" he cries.

"I want to do that!" Cole exclaims.

"It's called the 'Superman,'" says Jose.

"Let's focus on getting across the regular way for starters, Champ," advises Mom.

"Who will go first?" asks Jose. "What about you, senorita?" he turns to Valentina.

"Okay, sure," she says leaning back as Jose clamps her to the cable.

"Aieee!" Valentina shrieks as she zooms across the cable to meet Diego on the other side. She widely smiles as he snaps her photo with a portable camera.

"We take pictures for you to buy throughout the tour," says Jose.

"Valentina will love that," laughs Chloe.

She goes next and speeds over to the other side at about 35 miles per hour.

"Whee! That was fun! Come on, Sophie!" she grins and waves me to the other side.

"I want my turn!" Cole starts pouting, and I gladly step back to let him go.

His slide across the canopy is also uneventful, as is my mother's, who goes next.

"Ready, Sophie?" my father pushes me closer to the platform.

"I'm good. You can go now, Dad." I don't budge from the wooden waiting area bench.

"No, I want you to go before me, Sophie, because I don't want you to be the last one in the group here," Dad says.

"Get ready for the ride of your life, Chicita!" smiles Jose. "Gliding 400 feet over the glorious rainforest of Costa Rica!"

I shut my eyes as Jose clamps me on the zip line. I hope I don't wet my pants.

"Uno, dos, tres, cuatro!" he counts, then shoves me off the safety of the platform.

"Ahhhhhh!" I scream, and then look down at the trees below me. If I wasn't so scared of falling to my death, this might be fun. I see a bright blue and orange animal moving down below. It might be a parrot! I crane my neck to get a better look, then my body starts turning in the direction I came from.

What's happening?!

"Help! I'm going backward!!" I call.

In a reflex motion, I start moving my hands to the zip line cable.

"Don't touch the cable, senorita! You're fine!" I hear Diego shouting. "Just lean your body back."

"I can't do it!" I scream. "I'm going too fast."

"Lie down, Sophie! Lie down!" Valentina, Chloe, and my mother call.

It's hard with the cable moving so fast, but I lie back as far as I can and finally swing around to face my friends.

Diego uses his brake to help me stop, as I zoom toward the platform.

"You did it!" Chloe, Valentina, and my brother are smiling and Diego snaps of picture of my grimace as I land. Mom gives me a big hug.

"Great job, sweetie!"

"You looked like you were trying to do the Superman!" says Cole.

One zip down, nine more to go.

I loosen up after our third zip line and start having fun. It is cool to see all the trees and try to identify animals I see below.

"I saw three monkeys on my last zip," brags Chloe.

"We have four little monkeys up here." teases Mom.

Midway through the excursion, we race across a river.

"There are crocodiles down there!" Dad exclaims.

Cole goes last on the final platform and swings his arms out in the air.

"I'm superman!" he yells.

"Be careful, son!" shrieks Mom.

"You knew he would do it!" I laugh.

"Thanks for letting us go zip lining, Mr. Washington. That was so much fun!" enthuse my friends, after we make it back to the base camp area and order cool mango smoothies, while we wait for Jose to download our pictures.

The funniest one of me is the one from my first zip line, where my face is turned downward to scout out a parrot and my behind is in the air.

"Delete that one, Daddy!" I demand as everyone else laughs.

After we load back up into our minivan to make our way back to the hotel, we each reflect quietly on the day.

"I want to zip again," sighs Cole watching some howler monkeys swinging through the trees.

I wouldn't go that far. But we did have fun.

Chapter 10

Keep Away

"Last one in is a rotten egg!" teases Valentina as we do cannon ball jumps into the hotel pool.

After dozing a bit on our ride back from zip lining, we are full of energy and ready to enjoy the rest of our afternoon off. While Dad's in his hut reviewing medical charts of patients he'll be seeing tomorrow, we order fish tacos, burgers and fries by the pool.

"In the morning we'll be back at it at the mission," says Mom. "I think they want our group in the kitchen again, and Dad will be doing minor surgical procedures on people who have rotten teeth."

"Sophie might have to go too because she had cavities last year," teases Cole.

"Did not!" I say.

"Did too!" he responds flicking me with a beach towel.

"Sophie, Cole, that's enough!" my mother chastises us both.

"Maybe we'll see Agnese again," says Chloe, ignoring the ruckus.

"I hope, so, she was really nice, and it was interesting learning about how school is here in Costa Rica," adds Valentina.

Around 4 o'clock, Mom makes us get out of the water.

"We need to rest a bit before dinner, and I don't want you kids to get sunburned."

Mom takes Cole to his hut to help him get changed and make sure he doesn't disturb my father as he works.

"Stay in the hut, girls, and I'll get you in a couple of hours for dinner."

After we change out of our swimsuits, we sit and look at pictures Valentina has taken on the vacation with her phone.

"You could make a nice photo collage with these when we get home," I say.

"Yeah, my brother Hector and grandmother will enjoy seeing them," Valentina responds. "Abuela has always wanted to come to Costa Rica."

"You use Spanish words so often I'm starting to think they are English," laughs Chloe. "I called my grandma "abuela" last week!"

Tap, tap, tap.

A knocking sound at the door interrupts our conversation.

"Wonder who that is?" I ask. My mother and father have a key to our room and haven't been knocking when they come to get us.

I rush to the door peephole to look out but don't see anyone.

Tap, tap, tap, tap.

The noise gets louder.

"It's coming from the bottom of the door!" Valentina exclaims. She peers out the blinds to get a better view.

"The monkey is back! And look, Chloe, he's hitting on the door with your headband!"

"What!" Chloe exclaims, pulling the door open indignantly.

Eee! Eee! Eee! our visitor shrieks. The red barrette the monkey swiped from Chloe on its first visit is still dangling from the fur on its head, and it is holding the sparkly headband in its left paw.

"Give me my headband, you little thief!" Chloe squats and makes a grab for the hair decoration.

Ooo. Ooo. Eee! Eee! he cries again.

"Grab him!" Valentina shouts. I try to snatch the stolen goods from his paws but the monkey quickly jerks away. He backs toward the tall palm trees and we follow.

"You aren't getting away this time, mister!" Chloe responds.

We play a game of keep-away with the monkey for the next fifteen minutes, following him deeper and deeper into the jungle until, suddenly, he scampers off.

"Where did he go?!" Chloe turns around.

"I think he went to the left," I answer. "Or maybe he's in the bushes over here to the right. Here, monkey, monkey! Come here, monkey, monkey!"

He's vanished.

"Let's head back," suggests Valentina. "There are too many plants back here to see anything, and he's long gone by now."

We walk in circles for the next five minutes but aren't able to retrace our steps back to the hut. If anything, it feels like we're deeper in the jungle than when we started.

It's starting to get darker and the howler monkeys begin their nighttime song.

Ooo! Ooo! Ooo!

"We've got to get out of here!" says Chloe, sounding scared. "Did you bring your phone, Valentina?"

"I left it back in the room," she responds.

"Where is the path?!" I cry. "We can't stay here all night!"

Chapter 11

Scouts Honor

"I wish I hadn't dropped out of Girl Scouts last year," moaned Chloe. "My troop was working on their *Finding Your Way* badge."

"Eeeeek!"

She walks into an enormous spider web and wipes the sticky, silky material off her arm.

"Be careful, there might be a poisonous spider nearby," I warn.

I wonder what other animals are out here?

Before we came on our trip, my father told us that there are man-eating crocodiles in Costa Rica. At least we aren't near the water. But there could be snakes out here like that boa constrictor we saw on our first day.

I shiver as we cluster close together and take in our surroundings. It doesn't look like any people have been in this area recently. The plants are all overgrown, and you can't see a trail or footprints besides ours. There is a log on the ground from a fallen tree and mosquitoes are buzzing around everywhere. Wet and muddy, the rainforest has a damp, woodsy smell.

"We don't know the way back!" says Valentina in alarm. "What should we do?"

"My parents will realize we are gone soon and come looking for us," I reply. "I say we just wait here."

There's a rustling through the trees. I cover my eyes with my hands in terror.

"Never mind. Let's run, y'all!"

"Open your eyes, silly," commands Chloe, pulling my hands off my face, "it's just an iguana."

I peek and see a green mini version of a dinosaur, scurrying through the bush.

"But we do need to get out of here," Chloe continues. "Remember that cartoon *Dora the Explorer* we used to watch when we were little? They showed animals in the rainforest, and I distinctly remember that one was a jaguar. There are wild cats in the jungle, and they come out at night. We'll be safer if we can somehow find our way out of here before it gets too dark."

"If only we hadn't followed that silly monkey!" laments Valentina. "I'm sorry I left my phone, guys."

"You didn't know," I console her. "None of us did."

"Come on," commands Chloe, "let's get going."

We follow her and timidly try to retrace our steps.

"Did anybody drop anything?" I ask. "Maybe we will see something on the ground that can lead us back where we came from."

"I know that monkey was holding on to my headband tighter than tight," responds Chloe, "so that won't be on the ground."

"Hey, guys! I see something red over that way!" shouts Valentina.

"It's my barrette!" Chloe exclaims.

She picks it up and we continue trying to retrace our steps. I don't see anything else that looks familiar.

"It's useless!" says Chloe after we've rambled through the brush fifteen more minutes. "I feel even more lost than when we started."

"Don't give up yet," I urge. "I remember seeing that smaller palm tree when we came in here." I point out the tree and guide the other girls in that direction. A few more minutes of searching and I realize I was wrong.

Ooo! Ooo! Ooo! howl the monkeys. I'm more scared than I've ever been.

Maybe this was the area the monkey ran off to and not the path leading back to our hut.

"Let's stop for a minute so we don't wear ourselves out," suggests Valentina.

Chloe and I quit walking but we don't say anything.

My stomach rumbles. Mom should be coming to our hut by now to get us for dinner. I hope she finds us soon!

Chapter 12

Jungle Night

"What if we have to spend the night in the jungle?" cries Chloe, looking up at the darkening sky. "Something might eat us!!"

"There's got to be a way out of here," I answer.

"Your parents should definitely know we're gone by now," says Valentina. "They are probably getting a search party together."

I glance around to make sure no animals are sneaking up to attack us.

I'm especially nervous about seeing a snake. In science class last year, we learned that some snakes are nocturnal animals that sleep in the day and hunt for food at night. We probably look like three juicy steaks to a hungry boa constrictor.

A mosquito bites my arm, and I feel more tiny insects buzzing by my ear.

"These bugs are treacherous!" I slap them away as best I can.

"Yeah, I wish I'd sprayed on some bug repellant after I took my shower," moans Chloe.

I bite my lip to keep from crying. If only we'd listened to my mother and stayed in our room!

"Watch out!"

Valentina almost jumps out of her skin as she backs away from the tree she was leaning against. I look up and see an animal hugging on the tree trunk about five feet up. It is brown and furry with a long tail and has white face with black sloped down rings around its eyes. Its black mouth turns up like it's grinning at us.

"It's a tree sloth," whispers Chloe as we crouch together in fear. "Remember those slow-moving animals we saw in the movie *Zootopia*? I don't think they are dangerous."

I hope the sloth doesn't attack because it's fingernails are Guinness book long. He seems more curious than ferocious as he smiles down from the trees. A couple of minutes later, the sloth starts moving, and I exhale as he swings to a tree farther from where we're standing.

First *Dora the Explorer* and now a *Disney* movie have given us information out here in the wild. All our cartoon watching at home has made us animal experts. I'll have to mention this to my mother next time she fusses at me to turn off the TV.

When we stand still the mosquitoes are eating us alive, so we keep moving through the trees, hoping and praying we'll see something familiar.

"Maybe we should beat on something so they will hear where we are," I suggest as we pass another fallen tree.

"No. Making noise might attract animals hunting for food," Chloe warns.

I shiver from goosebumps of fear as the sun sets farther down and vibrant colors fill the sky. What looked glorious the other night at dinner now seems terrifying.

"I've got to use the bathroom!" exclaims Valentina.

"Can't you wait?" I hiss in fear and irritation.

"Until when?" she asks. "Who knows when someone will find us? I don't want to wet my pants out here and attract even more mosquitoes, or worse."

"Ewww!" Chloe squinches up her nose. "This is getting more terrible by the minute. Maybe you can go by that tree over there."

We move closer to the vines and turn our backs on our friend.

"Hurry up, Valentina," I urge.

I absently shift some vines away from my braids while we wait for Valentina to finish up.

It sounds like water is gushing from a faucet.

"I shouldn't have drunk so much water earlier," she says.

One of the vines keeps moving, and I swat at it again. It is cold and scaly, and suddenly I realize what I'm touching is not a plant.

"Ahhhhh!" I screech. "A snake!!"

I recoil and the small, green serpent continues hanging from the vines. I close my eyes, hoping this will be a dream, like the nightmare I had of the boa constrictor the other night.

But when I open them, the snake is still on the vine flicking out its tongue and easing closer to my head.

"Run, Sophie!" yells Valentina, zipping up her shorts. Chloe yanks on my t-shirt and I follow.

"Mom! Dad! Help us!" I call, heedless of the unseen dangers.

"Help! Help!" echo Chloe and Valentina.

"Heeeelp!!!"

My heart pounds as fast as a bongo drum as we rush through the black night, praying that someone hears our calls.

Chapter 13

Found

I see a dim light, shining in the darkness.

"Sophie, Chloe, Valentina," comes a faint call.

"Mom! Dad! Over here!" I yell even louder than I cheer with our squad at our school basketball games.

"Mr. and Mrs. Washington! We're here!" echo my friends.

A few minutes later, I'm wrapped up in my father's arms, crying tears of relief.

A man in a hotel uniform is standing with my father, holding a flashlight and a gun.

"What possessed you girls to come out here?" Dad scolds after grabbing all three of us up in a group hug.

Chloe explains about the monkey at our door.

"I'm sorry, Dad," I reply. "We didn't realize we had run so far. We were so busy worrying about getting Chloe's headband back that we didn't think."

"It is a good thing we found you girls before it got completely dark out here," says the hotel guide. "That is when many of the jungle animals come out to hunt."

"I know," I reply. "We saw a tree sloth and a small snake."

"What!" exclaims my father. "I guess we should blame ourselves for leaving you unsupervised for so long. Please follow my instructions carefully for the rest of the trip and promise me you'll never run off again without an adult. We are responsible not only for your well-being, Sophie, but that of your friends, whose parents have entrusted us to care for them on this trip."

"We're sorry, Mr. Washington," Chloe and Valentina say remorsefully.

"I'm so glad you girls are safe." My father cuddles me close to him as we walk back to the hut.

"Sophie Washington, you had me scared to death!" My mother wraps me in her arms then wipes away tears as we approach the hut.

"Hey, guys, what's up?" asks Cole cheerfully.

Dad shares the news about our monkey business, and Mom gives us a second scolding.

I feel bad about disobeying my parents.

"I don't ever want to see another monkey again, even in the zoo!" Chloe declares.

"This place is filled with monkeys, so good luck with that," responds my father, lightening the mood.

"I wish I'd had a key to lock you girls inside the hut when I left," says Mom. "But I won't make that mistake again."

"Leaving them locked in the hut with no way out would be just as unsafe as having them unsupervised," responds Dad. "What if there is an emergency and they need to leave?"

"What kind of key opens a banana?" interrupts Cole. "A monkey!"

I'm so happy to be back with my family that I don't complain about Cole's corny jokes or my parent's not trusting me and treating me and my friends like babies.

Mom stays in our hut with us as we shower and get dressed for dinner. I put on a sundress and grab a light sweater in case the air conditioning is on high in the restaurant.

"You sure you girls are okay?" She watches in concern as we comb our hair and rub ointment on our bug bites.

"Yes, ma'am," we respond as we walk back to join my father and Cole. I'm just happy to be found.

Once we enter Bananas, the nicer restaurant in the hotel complex, my father gives the hostess our name so we can be seated. We wait our turn to get a table, and I admire the dark wood walls and lacy white table cloths. It seems like the scary jungle we were just lost in is a world away. Lighted candles gleam throughout the darkened room and each table has a vase filled with various tropical flowers.

"Hola, and welcome to Bananas," says our server, a short pretty lady with large, dark eyes and a small red flower tucked over her ear. "May I take your order?"

We try another local dish with beans, rice, and fish.

"They sure do eat a lot of beans around here," says Chloe, taking a bite. "But this is good. I'm so hungry after running around in the jungle that I could eat an entire pan."

"Me too, agrees Valentina, spearing a piece of fish with her fork.

"I like the burgers we had at lunch better," says Cole.

"You would," I laugh.

As sip from my water glass, I spy something moving near the wood beams in the ceiling. *Is that what I think it is?* I nudge Chloe under the table.

"Look up there," I point.

"What do you see?" she whispers.

A long black tail moves near the ceiling and I feel goosebumps rise on my arms.

"Hey, tell me the secret." Valentina leans over to see what's going on, then pulls out her cell phone to try to take a picture.

"It's a rat!" I jump out of my seat.

"Sophie! Pipe down!" says my father from across the table. "You'll disturb all the other people in the restaurant."

If I were them I would want to be disturbed, so I wouldn't eat anything else in here. And this is supposed to be a fancy restaurant!

My father stands to get a closer look at the creature. "Actually, I think it may be a young raccoon."

"Raccoon! We're going to get sick!" I exclaim, holding my stomach. The animal moves into the light and I recognize the black bandit-like mask on its face and see that it's long tail is furry and ringed.

"Don't get so upset, Sophie," my mother consoles. "He's not in the kitchen. Since this place is in the middle of the jungle, it's probably difficult to keep wild animals out."

"Remember when that raccoon got in our attic at home last year?" recalls Cole. "We thought there was an alien up there until the pest control man trapped him."

The raccoon scampers off out of sight before anyone else in the restaurant sees it.

"No wonder they keep it so dark in here!" I exclaim.

"We'll certainly have lots of animals to talk about when we get back to school," laughs Chloe.

Thankfully, we are pretty much done with our meal, so I don't have to wonder what may be mixed in with my food as I eat.

Our server returns to the table. "Would you care for dessert?"

"No, thank you," my mother responds, and we all smile.

Chapter 14

The Fence

Our next day in the village isn't as exciting as our first two. We are back in the kitchen, but Agnese and her mother don't join us.

"I guess she had to go to school today," says Valentina, glancing around for our new friend.

"Agnese is in a soccer tournament in a nearby town," says Greta, the mission coordinator. "You may see her again tomorrow."

We spend most of the morning slicing huge mounds of onions and peppers. Cole is back washing dishes and it looks more like he is taking a swim than cleaning pots and pans.

"You have to admit, this is better than hauling buckets of water in the sun," he says, splashing in the soapy water.

"I never want to see another onion again in my life!" I whine.

"I know, right," agrees Chloe. "We smell terrible."

"Just think about all the villagers you are helping," reminds Mom. "The food we are prepping allows the ladies to get other needed work done in the community and feeds the mission volunteers as well."

After a lunch of sandwiches, plantain chips and mixed fruit, Greta leads us to a small brick house in another area of town.

"This fence needs a new coat of paint," she says bringing up some buckets and brushes. "If you can finish up this afternoon that would be great."

"I wonder why the people who live here don't paint their own fence," I grumble as I dip my brush in the bucket of paint for the hundredth time.

My shoulders and back are sore, and the sun is hotter than ever.

"They should have started us on this in the morning," Valentina agrees. We are all dripping wet, and Valentina's face is red.

"That would have been a good idea," says my mother, pulling her sweat soaked hair back in a ponytail holder, "but I'm sure Greta has a reason for having us work here. Cole and Chloe, why don't you put your caps back on?"

It has to be at least ninety-five degrees out here in the shade, and the fence is almost as tall as my father. We have to stand on our tiptoes to paint the top portions. The heat combined with the fumes from the paint is making me queasy. *We'll never get done by our usual quitting time!*

"Mommy, my arms are tired," complains Cole.

"Let's take a water break," my mother suggests, "and we'll finish up what we can before 4 p.m."

"I can't believe how tired I am," groans Chloe. "Painting a fence is hard work."

"Yeah, they make it seem like fun in the story, *Tom Sawyer*," says Cole.

Around two o'clock, Greta brings out three stepstools for us to use.

"I noticed you were having some technical difficulties," she says, watching Cole strain to paint an upper corner of the fence.

"Thank you, this is much better," I say, standing on one of the stoops.

"We did it!" Valentina exclaims two hours later as she swipes white paint on the last portion of the fence and rubs paint off her chin.

"Another great job, kids!" Mom gives us each a mini high-five. "See what you can do when you put your minds to it?"

We stand back to admire our work. While we are gathering up our materials, an elderly woman approaches from the village, stops and stares at the restored fence in surprise and widely smiles.

"No lo puedo creer!" she exclaims, teary-eyed. "Gracias, niños."

"Gracias!" we reply as the woman continues to talk quickly in Spanish.

"She says she can't believe it," translates Valentina. "She's wanted the fence painted since her husband died two years ago, but she lives alone and the men in the town have been so busy with other work they couldn't help her."

The woman, whose name is Senora Hernandez, gestures for us to wait as she goes in the house and returns with a plate of sweet churros and ice-cold bottles of water, and gives us each a hug.

I beam.

Though I'm sticky and sweaty in the heat, it feels good to help someone else.

Chapter 15

Mission Accomplished

Friday is our last day working for the mission. We help move bricks behind the clinic building while my dad sees patients inside.

"These will be used to build special storage area for supplies," Greta explains.

Two other women from the village join us as we pick up the three-pound bricks and stones. They don't speak English, but Valentina answers their questions about where we are from and how we came to help at the mission.

"This trip convinces me that I need to take a Spanish class or get some Spanish language audiotapes to learn from in the car after we get home," says my mother. "There are too many Spanish speaking people back home in Houston that we interact with daily for us not the learn the language. Many of your dad's patients that we see in his dental office are native Spanish speakers and so are the landscape people we use to cut our grass."

"Tacos, por favor?" Cole asks the villagers for lunch after we've been at it for about three hours.

They laugh and point at a food truck that is driving down the street.

"I've never worked so hard in my life!" exclaims Chloe, as we sit under a coconut tree to eat the fresh fish and meat tacos my mother buys.

"Yeah, we'll need a vacation from our vacation when we get back home," jokes Valentina.

"We don't return until Sunday morning," Mom answers. "Your father has a fun activity planned for us to do tomorrow since it's our last day here."

Dad looks exhausted but happy when we meet him in the clinic area to catch our minibus to the hotel later that afternoon.

"We've been able to help a lot of people this week," he says, sliding off his white work jacket.

"Thank you all for your hard work." Greta comes to meet us before we head back. "It's special that you children came to do this on your school holiday. I hope it's been a memorable experience."

"There's definitely no way we will forget this vacation!" agrees Valentina.

"Oh, and before I forget, Mrs. Alvarez left this for you this morning," Greta holds out an envelope.

It's a letter from Agnese!

Dear Friends,

I am so happy to meet you and learn about American life. I hope I can travel one day to Houston, Texas to see your home. I am sorry that I could not see you again, but Mami says I need to learn my school lessons well if I want to attend college in the U.S.

Please write back soon and send pictures.
Your Friend,
Agnese

Inside the envelope is a picture of Agnese in her black and white soccer uniform. The photo must be from when she was younger because her straight black hair is cut in a shorter bob than it is now and one of her front teeth is missing. I hold the letter close. It will be fun to send our new friend pen pal letters and emails when we get home. Maybe one day she can come visit us back in Houston.

Before we leave we stop by the pottery area to buy souvenirs. Chloe chooses a large vase with a monkey swinging from a coconut tree with green leaves carved on it. Valentina buys a similar sized vase that has a large butterfly carving and is colored rust, black and brown, and I pick a blue wall hanging with an iguana design.

"You should have picked one with a snake drawing," teases Cole.

He watches in amazement as a man spins a bowl around on the pottery wheel.

"Can I get one of those for Christmas?" he asks my mother. "They might sell them at the craft store."

My brother's eyes get even bigger when he sees how much money Dad counts out to pay for the pottery.

"Here you go, thirty dollars each."

"If I get my own pottery wheel, I could make things and sell them for money. You could retire from your dental office, Dad!"

"We'll see about that, son," my father chuckles.

Senora Hernandez is sitting on her porch as we drive by. She points at her freshly painted fence and smiles and waves at us, and we wave back.

The area where people were lined up to get checkups at the clinic is empty.

"We saw almost one hundred patients this week," says Dad. "I'm glad we had the chance to help so many."

It's been a crazy week, but our mission to be of service has been accomplished.

Chapter 16

River Cruise

We sleep in the next morning. After we'd returned to our huts from Guaitil, we played at the beach until nightfall then had a nice dinner back at the hotel restaurant. We stayed up until late in the evening playing ping pong and dance video games in the hotel's game room. Happily, none of our jungle friends returned to disturb us during the night.

"I kind of miss that crazy monkey," says Chloe, clasping on her found red barrette in the mirror. "Though I do wish he would return my favorite headband."

"You're just as loco as the monkey is!" exclaims Valentina. "I can't believe you'd put that back in your hair after that wild animal had it in its fur!"

"I washed it in the sink, so it should be okay. Right, Mrs. W?"

"There shouldn't be any problem with wearing your barrette, Chloe," agrees my mother. "Come on, girls. Let's go join the guys outside so we can go on our excursion."

"We've had so much excitement on this trip that I'd be just as happy spending the day at the beach or shopping in town for more souvenirs," I say.

"I know what you mean," says my mother. "But your father and I planned this excursion before we came on the trip. It will be a neat experience."

"What are we doing?" I ask.

"We're going on a river cruise!" shouts Cole, overhearing the question. "And we might see real live crocodiles."

"That is a definite," says my father. "The river we'll be riding in is filled with them."

Cole is jumping up and down in excitement. "I brought my camera so I can take pictures like you do, Valentina."

I just shake my head.

The idea of my hyper little brother in a river overflowing with man eating crocodiles doesn't sound like a good idea to me. But just like I did with the zip lining, I roll with it. Mom and Dad are the parents here.

"After we do our river boat tour, we'll stop in a nearby village for lunch," says my mother.

"Sounds like a great plan," answers Dad.

The ride to the river area is even bumpier than the one we took to Guaitil.

"Whooa!" I hold on to my seat to keep from bouncing out of it.

"In the rainy season these roads are full of mud and impossible to drive through," says our guide.

He points out a parrot in a nearby tree and stops so we can take pictures.

"I got a close up!" Cole broadcasts.

"Maybe you can be a pottery maker and a photographer," I joke.

The riverboat we get in seats fifteen people, which is not as big as I expected. It has a canopy overhead to shield us from the roasting sun.

"What if a crocodile tips this thing over?" I whisper to Dad.

"We'd better swim fast," he laughs.

The boat takes off and I take a seat in the middle, away from the edge.

"Look, Chloe! Your friend might be with his family!" Valentina points out a group of capuchin monkeys hanging from a tree on the riverbank. Our boat edges close to the bank, and one of the monkeys jumps on the top of the seat in front of Chloe.

"Oh my goodness!" my mother exclaims.

"I think he wants your barrette back," I giggle.

"These capuchins come here each day for food," explains the captain, handing the primate a small banana, which it grabs and hops back to the bank.

Farther down the river, a family of iguanas sun themselves. The guide also points out interesting birds and enormous insects along the way.

"That thing's head is huge." Cole motions to a crocodile moving through the river on the other side of the boat.

"Wow! I've never seen anything like it in the wild!" says Dad. He takes a picture with his camera and Valentina leans in to take a selfie of her and Chloe with her phone, while I hang back.

"Come on and join us!" they urge.

"No thanks," I say. I'm not trying to be an afternoon snack.

Cole pouts as he checks his camera to review the digital photos he took.

"My pictures are all blurry."

"Don't worry, dear, I'm sure we'll see another one," Mom reassures him.

A few minutes later, another crocodile with an even bigger mouth than the one we saw earlier swims near our boat.

"Watch this," says the boat operator. He pulls a huge piece of raw chicken out of a bag and holds it over the edge of the boat.

Seconds later, the crocodile rises up out of the water and exposes a mouth full of sharp teeth and a head as big as over half my body.

"Watch, guys, I'm going to get a great picture of this!" shouts my brother.

"Cole, step back!" yells my mother in alarm.

Cole ignores her and leans dangerously close to the edge, trying to snap a picture. Then he wobbles.

"Oh, no! I'm falling!!" he calls.

Chapter 17

Tick Tock

My father pulls my brother from the edge of the boat. But Cole loses his grip on his camera and it slides into the mouth of the hungry crocodile.

"My pictures!" he wails.

"Don't ever pull a stunt like that again, young man," Dad scolds sharply. "These are wild animals, not pets."

"Cole is probably too young to take on an outing like this," says my mother.

My brother starts to cry.

"Now I won't have any pictures from the trip."

"I'll send you copies of mine, Cole," soothes Valentina.

Things calm down as we continue down the river, and we spy several other crocodiles resting on the riverside and easing through the water.

Valentina takes shots of Cole posing with the creatures in the background and promises to make printouts for him.

"I wonder if they'll see a photo light flash from the mouth of the crocodile that ate my camera the next time the tour guides feed it chicken," asks Cole. "It would be like that crocodile from the story *Peter Pan* that started making the 'Tick Tock' sound after he gobbled up Captain Hook's watch."

"Let's hope not," I answer, "because that would mean the crocodile who got your camera would want to eat your hand like Tick Tock did Captain Hook's."

"You have a wild imagination, Cole," chuckles my father.

Once the river boat tour is over, the van driver takes us to a small village for lunch.

"What a day!" exclaims my mother, tucking into her plantains.

"Yeah, traveling with the Washington family is a thrill a minute," laughs Chloe.

"If I come here again, I'd like to go deep sea fishing or white water rafting," says Dad.

"Cole will have to be a year or two older before we try that," my mother replies.

"Eight is plenty old!" Cole protests.

"Well, maybe you'll have to prove to us that you can listen better," mom responds. "because my nerves are shot after seeing you leaning near the edge of the boat near a hungry crocodile."

"I got a great picture of it," says Valentina, showing us the photo from her phone.

The crocodile's open mouth looks humungous, and I shiver seeing how close Cole was to his razor sharp teeth.

"Wow, that looks like something out of *National Geographic* magazine!" my father exclaims.

"You take pictures so often that maybe you might be photographer one day, Valentina," I say.

"Yeah, I saw a free class at the library on digital photography that I might sign up for this summer," she agrees.

After we return to our hotel, we make our way to the pool for a final swim.

"This has been a great vacation, Sophie," says Chloe. "Thanks so much for inviting us."

"Even our time getting lost in the jungle together seems cool, now that we're safe," agrees Valentina.

"It wouldn't have been half as fun without you two here," I reply. "I'd have been stuck in a room with Cole whining all night and have to listen to his corny jokes all day."

"I think he's funny and so cute," says Chloe. "You're probably just used to him because he's your little brother and around all the time."

"I feel the same way about my little brother, Hector," says Valentina. "That boy can really drive me nuts, but this week I *have* missed him."

We relax in our hut after dinner and scroll through Valentina's phone to look at all her photos.

"Remember to forward all the group pictures of us to me, and please don't forget the one with Cole and the crocodile," I say.

"He'd have a fit if I didn't send you a copy of that one," Valentina agrees.

Surprisingly, my mother trusts us to stay in the room on our own on our last night, and she is bunking with Cole and Dad in the other hut. We play cards again and then gossip about girls and boys in our class.

At midnight, we turn off the lights.

"Goodnight, Sophie."

"Goodnight, Chloe and Valentina."

I dream about floating down a gentle river lined with coconut and banana trees. It's not too hot, and leaves from the trees sway in a gentle breeze.

Chapter 18

Monkey See, Monkey Do

Tap. Tap. Tap.

Around one in the morning, a sound wakes me. I sit up in bed.

"Chloe, Valentina, do you hear something?" I whisper.

"Is it time to get up? Did we miss our plane?" Chloe stretches and mumbles sleepily.

"No, I hear that noise again," I call.

Tap. Tap. Tap.

Ooo! Ooo! Ooo!

"We have a visitor on our last night!"

"Let me see," says Chloe.

Instead of flicking on the lights, she tiptoes to the door and slowly slides it open.

There sits the monkey, holding Chloe's sparkly headband in its paw.

I blink my eyes and he blinks his. Chloe raises her right hand. The monkey raises his left paw. I scratch my nose; the monkey rubs his.

"He's copying us!" Chloe exclaims, standing on one foot to see if the monkey will do the same.

He does, and it's a game of monkey see, monkey do the next couple of minutes as the primate imitates every move we make.

"Gotcha!" Chloe abruptly stops our follow the leader game and grabs her headpiece.

Eee! Eee! Eee!

The monkey shrieks, angrily.

Valentina joins us at the door and turns on the outside light.

Startled, the monkey turns and scampers off into the jungle.

"We've been getting up nearly every night on this trip with that monkey," sighs Valentina, rubbing her eyes. "I'll be glad to get home to get a good night's sleep."

"I'm happy I have my headband," says Chloe. I wonder why that tricky little monkey kept coming back?"

"He had a mission just like we did at the village," I giggle. "To make sure our trip was as exciting as possible."

"Well, I'd say he did a great job," laughs Valentina.

My friends and I are sleepy the next morning and are quiet in the airport as we wait for our plane. Cole, on the other hand, is well rested and hops around like a Mexican jumping bean.

"Mom! Dad! Can we buy some extra snacks for the plane?" he asks. "I want some gummy bears. I can't wait to see our dog, Bertram! Wonder what he's been doing?"

"Hopefully, not chewing up all of Mr. McEwan's shoes like he does ours at home," laughs Dad. "Let's settle down, son. It's too early to eat candy."

We board the plane, and Valentina, Chloe and I are in the same row. Once we stow our bags into the overhead compartments, my friends snuggle in their seats with throw blankets to nap.

I'm tired too, but I'm too giddy about going home to fall back to sleep. I raise up the blind from my window seat and watch as we soar above the trees, leaving our vacation spot behind. I can't wait to tell Mariama about our trip! She missed out by going to Disney World instead. *Adios, Costa Rica! Hope I can return one day.*

Dear Reader:

Thank you for reading *Sophie Washington: Mission Costa Rica*, the sixth book in my Sophie Washington series! I hope you liked it. If you enjoyed the book, I'd be grateful if you post a short review on Amazon. Your feedback really makes a difference and helps others learn about my books. I appreciate your support!

Tonya

Books by
Tonya Duncan Ellis

For information on all Tonya Duncan Ellis books about Sophie and her friends

Check out the following pages!

You'll find:

• Blurbs about the other exciting books in the Sophie Washington series

• Information about Tonya Duncan Ellis

Sophie Washington: Queen of the Bee

Sign up for the spelling bee?

No way!

If there's one thing 10-year-old Texan Sophie Washington is good at, it's spelling. She's earned straight 100s on all her spelling tests to prove it. Her parents want her to compete in the Xavier Academy spelling bee, but Sophie wishes they would buzz off.

Her life in the Houston suburbs is full of adventures, and she doesn't want to slow down the action. Where else can you chase wild hogs out of your yard, ride a bucking sheep, or spy an eight-foot-long alligator during a bike ride through the neighborhood? Studying spelling words seems as fun as getting stung by a hornet, in comparison.

That's until her irritating classmate, Nathan Jones, challenges her. There's no way she can let Mr. Know-It-All win. Studying is hard when you have a pesky younger brother and a busy social calendar. Can Sophie ignore the distractions and become Queen of the Bee?

Sophie Washington:
The Snitch

There's nothing worse than being a tattletale...

That's what 10-year-old Sophie Washington thinks until she runs into Lanie Mitchell, a new girl at school. Lanie pushes Sophie and her friends around at their lockers, and even takes their lunch money.

If they tell, they are scared the other kids in their class will call them snitches and won't be their friends. And when you're in the fifth grade, nothing seems worse than that.

Excitement at home keeps Sophie's mind off the trouble with Lanie.

She takes a fishing trip to the Gulf of Mexico with her parents and little brother, Cole, and discovers a mysterious creature in the attic above her room. For a while, Sophie is able to keep her parents from knowing what is going on at school. But Lanie's bullying goes too far, and a classmate gets seriously hurt. Sophie needs to make a decision. Should she stand up to the bully, or become a snitch?

Sophie Washington: Things You Didn't Know About Sophie

Oh, the tangled web we weave...

Sixth grader Sophie Washington thought she had life figured out when she was younger, but this school year, everything changed. She feels like an outsider because she's the only one in her class without a cell phone, and her crush, new kid Toby Johnson, has been calling her best friend Chloe. To fit in, Sophie changes who she is. Her plan to become popular works for a while, and she and Toby start to become friends.

In between the boy drama, Sophie takes a whirlwind class field trip to Austin, TX, where she visits the state museum, eats Tex-Mex food, and has a wild ride on a kayak. Back at home, Sophie fights off buzzards from her family's roof, dissects frogs in science class, and has fun at her little brother Cole's basketball tournament.

Things get more complicated when Sophie "borrows" a cell phone and gets caught. If her parents make her tell the truth, what will her friends think? Turns out Toby has also been hiding something, and Sophie discovers the best way to make true friends is to be yourself.

Sophie Washington: The Gamer

40 Days Without Video Games? Oh No!

Sixth-grader Sophie Washington and her friends are back with an interesting book about having fun with video games while keeping balance. It's almost Easter, and Sophie and her family get ready to start fasts for Lent with their church, where they give up doing something for 40 days that may not be good for them. Her parents urge Sophie to stop tattling so much and encourage her second-grade brother Cole to give up something he loves most, playing video games. The kids agree to the challenge, but how long can they keep it up? Soon after Lent begins, Cole starts sneaking to play his video games. Things start to get out of control when he loses a school electronic tablet he checked out without his parents' permission and comes to his sister for help. Should Sophie break her promise and tattle on him?

Sophie Washington: Hurricane

#Sophie Strong

A hurricane's coming, and eleven-year-old Sophie Washington's typical middle school life in the Houston, Texas suburbs is about to make a major change. One day she's teasing her little brother, Cole, dodging classmate Nathan Jones' wayward science lab frog and complaining about "braggamuffin" cheerleader Valentina Martinez, and the next, she and her family are fleeing for their lives to avoid dangerous flood waters. Finding a place to stay isn't easy during the disaster, and the Washington's get some surprise visitors when they finally do locate shelter. To add to the trouble, three members of the Washington family go missing during the storm, and new friends lose their home. In the middle of it all, Sophie learns to be grateful for what she has and that she is stronger than she ever imagined.

About the Author

Tonya Duncan Ellis is author of the Sophie Washington book series which includes: *Queen of the Bee, The Snitch, Things You Didn't Know About Sophie, The Gamer, Hurricane* and *Mission: Costa Rica*. When she's not writing, she enjoys reading, swimming, biking and travel. She's visited Costa Rica but never had a monkey visit her hotel. Tonya lives in Houston, TX with her husband and three children.

Made in the USA
Middletown, DE
18 November 2020